# Spell Shaper

## Sarah Aghajanian

Illustrated by

Sara Slaybaugh

and Zivia Avalin

## DEDICATION

For all of my Miquon students.

# Author's Note

I set out to write a chapter book that would be fun for anyone to read, but that would have tools for older children with **dyslexia**..

When dyslexic people read, letters and words on a page can get mixed up and confusing. It has nothing to do with being smart! Some people are left handed, some people can snap their fingers, and some people are dyslexic. Every brain is different.

One of my students, Zivia Avelin, is an amazing writer and artist. She also has dyslexia. She read over the book with me and helped me to make sure that most of the words were either words children could sound out (like **mishap**) or were **sight words** (a word like **thought**). Right now, when most books are given a reading grade level, people usually only look at how many words are in each sentence. They do not even care what words the author used! This means that even some picture books are very hard to read and even harder to understand. As a reading teacher, this is shocking to my students and me. Here are some of the other ways Spell Shaper is more readable than most chapter books its size.

- Few contractions (words like **don't** and **didn't**)
- Many short sentences
- Cream paper instead of white
- Sans serif font, which helps dyslexic readers
- 14 point, larger font
- No italic type
- Single space after punctuation
- Larger line spacing
- No justified text
- Illustrations

Zivia also decided what all of the characters in the story should look like. She drew two of the pictures and my partner teacher Sara drew all the rest based on Zivia's plans. We hope you enjoy our book. We had a great time putting it all together.

-Sarah Aghajanian, M.S.Ed.

\*\*\*\*\*\*\*\*\*\*\*\*\*\*\*\*\*\*\*\*\*\*\*\*\*\*\*\*\*\*\*\*\*\*

# CONTENTS

# ACKNOWLEDGMENTS

I would like to thank the entire Miquon School community, for accepting each other for who we are while challenging one another to learn and grow.

I would like to thank Sara for being the best partner teacher I could hope for and an amazing artist to boot, and I would like to thank Zivia for sharing her gifts with us in the classroom and in this book. You are an inspiration to all of us.

Finally, I would like to thank my dear husband for all of his love and support with this project.

# ◀ Chapter 1 ▶

Finn woke up on the day of the fire test. He still could not get the spell to work. One last time, he shut his eyes and stretched out his hands. Gritting his teeth, he thought the words of the spell, over and over. He had done this about a hundred times the night before. But maybe, he hoped, this will be it. This will be the time that changes everything.

A buzzing feeling ran up and down his hands, like someone was sticking them with needles. He saw a crackling red fire in his mind. It began to warm his whole body. He was getting lost in the spell, and in the picture of the blazing fire. He let himself be swept away into the fire itself.

This is it, he thought. This is finally it!

But then, all at once, everything fell away. The words mixed themselves up until they were just a string of strange sounds.

The picture of the fire had vanished. His hands felt cold. Even before he opened his eyes, he knew that they were empty.

He did not try the spell again. There was no point.

Instead he grabbed a pillow and threw it as hard as he could across the room. Something yelped from behind his curtains. He blinked. His sister Star stuck out her head.

"That was mean, Finn!" she called.

"Why are you in my room?" Finn asked angrily. "Get out!"

"I have a new spell I wanted to show you," Star said. "But you woke up before I could surprise you."

Finn jumped off the bed and grabbed the Star-shaped lump. He shook it a little. It yelled.

"Ow! You don't have to get so mad about it, Finn! I was going to fill your room with sunshine. It's always so dark in here," Star complained.

He let her go. She pulled back the curtain and stepped out.

Finn scowled at her. "Can't you just wake me up normally?" he asked.

"I thought you could use a little help today. You don't look so good, by the way," Star said. "Maybe you should try to get more sleep." Then she dashed out of the room. Her annoying pink sneakers flashed blue with each step. She had learned to cast that spell in about ten seconds.

"Thanks a lot!" Finn yelled after her.

"You're welcome!" Star called out happily, as if she had really done him a nice thing.

Finn grabbed his pillow and threw it at a wall. It was not fair. He was the only ten-year-old in his school who was not able to do any magic yet. Star was almost as good with magic as the teachers. So far, she could do any spell that her class had learned, but Finn could not get a single one to work. My parents picked the right name for her, he thought, unhappily. She was the star of their magic school. He was only "Star's brother." And he was two years older! It was too embarrassing for words.

He checked the mirror to see if Star had been right. Of course she had. She was always right about everything. Deep gray bags hung under his eyes. He rubbed at them, but they were not going anywhere. His hair was sticking out in all directions, so he picked up a brush and attacked it. Finally it fell to his shoulders.

Like most elf men and boys, Finn liked to keep his hair long. His father had, too, when he was still alive.

Finn had once tried to use a spell to change his brown eyes to a more interesting color. But of course nothing had happened. Star had eyes like the river during a storm - powerful swirls of blue and green. His looked like the mud left over after the storm.

"Time for school, my boy!" called his mother from the kitchen downstairs. Finn frowned as he dressed in his school clothes. Today he picked leather pants and a dark blue shirt. Every shirt in his closet was blue, black, or grey. Anything else might make people notice him. If there was one thing Finn hated, it was to be noticed.

Finn walked slowly down the stairs. With each step, he tapped the wall with his fist. He was always doing things like that. Like when he walked under the old bridge he had to hold his breath. And on the way home from school he counted backwards from 50. They had started out as little games he played with himself. Sometimes he had tried to stop himself from playing them, but he never could. He worried that something bad might happen if he stopped. He had never told anyone about them, not even his mother. She did not need anything else to worry about.

Anyway, they were just silly games.

Something that smelled delicious was sizzling loudly. His aunt and uncle were helping his mother cook. They banged pots and pans as they worked.

"Pancakes?" he asked.

His aunt laughed. "I knew that would get you out of bed!"

His uncle got a plate and piled it high with food. He winked and handed it to Finn. He whispered, "We gave you two extras. Don't tell your sister or there will be a fight."

Finn nodded and dug into his food. His aunt and uncle were amazing cooks. His aunt flipped eggs and more pancakes in the pan. "Is the fire test today?" she asked.

She was pretending that she was not very interested, but Finn knew better. He had heard his family whispering about him late last night. They used words like **different** and **slow**. These were the same words the teachers wrote on his report cards. The ink and paper were all protected with spells. No student could change a grade. You could not destroy them either, not by ripping them or hammering them or burning them.

Finn had tried.

"Yes, the test is today. They should just fail me now. It would save everyone a lot of time."

"Finn," she scolded. "One of these days it is all going to make sense. Today could be the day."

"You say that every day."

His uncle patted Finn's arm. "One of these days it will be true. Keep your chin up, Finn. You know that your father had some trouble at first. I was not a perfect student myself. It runs in the family. Just keep working hard and don't give up."

Finn just grumbled and ate the last of his pancakes. He knew that the nice thing to do was to smile and nod, but he was too tired to be nice. He had heard it all for years. And it felt even worse when people talked about his father. It just made Finn miss him more.

His mother and Star came in from the dining room. Mother had somehow smoothed Star's wild, curly hair into two neat braids. She kissed both children on the cheek and handed them their school bags. "Be nice to one another," she warned. "And have a good day."

# ◄ Chapter 2 ►

Star jabbered on and on as they walked to school. She mostly talked about her classroom job. She had to clean out the pen of the school's two sheep, Bobo and Zodo. It was by far the worst classroom job. No one ever wanted it. Children tried all kinds of tricks to make some other poor kid have to do it. For some reason Star actually **liked** it. Finn was not surprised that every week she always seemed to be doing it. **She** was that poor kid.

"They make such a big mess that I get to use the mopping spell!"

"The mopping spell. Great," Finn mumbled. He was not really listening. But then she started to talk about her own test. That got his attention.

"Miss Bray said most of us won't be able to do it the first time. What if I forget everything?"

Finn wanted to scream. Then he wanted Star to play the Quiet Game. At least he always won at that. But instead he bit down hard on his lip.

She is not **trying** to annoy you, he told himself. She just loves school. If magic were that easy for you, you probably would too. Before Star came to school, Finn had never been a jealous person. When he was little and he saw children playing with their fathers, he sometimes felt a kind of longing. He was always happy for the children, though. He was never angry at what they had. He just missed his own father.

But all that changed the day he picked Star up from kindergarten. On that day he felt something totally different. He was walking down the hall from his classroom when he heard someone say his name. He peeked his head around the corner. Star's teacher, Miss Calla, was talking to the principal. Miss Calla had been his kindergarten teacher, too. That was the year that all of his problems with magic began. It had been upsetting for him, but Miss Calla had been so nice about it. She always smiled and said that it did not matter at all. Then she would slip him chocolates and treats when no one was looking.

Miss Calla was saying, "Thank goodness Star does not have Finn's needs. He is such a sweet boy, but in all of my years I have never seen someone have as hard a time as he does with magic. They say he still has not learned a single spell. Is that right?"

The principal said something too low for Finn to hear.

"Well, thank goodness Star is so bright. I feel so badly for poor Finn."

From that day on, Finn understood what everyone thought of him. Poor Finn was all he was. It was all he was ever going to be. After that, he walked away whenever he saw Miss Calla. She did not seem to care.

Star was still chattering on next to Finn as they walked through the forest path. Finn kicked at one of the many clumps of mushrooms that grew along the dirt road. The hunk of mushrooms flew into the air. It landed far away, next to a huge blue-bark tree. Finn was a little impressed at his kick, but Star did not even look up.

It was like she was just talking to herself. "I think Pennell is going to do better than I am, because she's a fairy. Everyone knows that fairies are always better with air magic than elves are." Finn rolled his eyes and kicked at another mushroom clump. It flew even farther. Finn smiled a little to himself. He might be horrible at magic, but he could kick a ball farther than almost anyone.

Around them, the forest was just waking up. Light was coming through the trees and animals were talking to one another. No one, no matter how rich or powerful, could live far from nature. It was where the real magic lived. You could not actually see the magic, of course. When Finn was little he had tried to look for it. He had picked up rocks and dug under tree roots. His mother once told him, "There are some things we can't see, but they are there all the same." Then she added, "And there are some things we think we see, but they are not there at all."

Finn still did not understand what she meant, but he knew deep inside that it was something important. Every now and then he thought about it. Maybe one day he would understand.

Star was still talking. "I mean, what if Miss Bray only gives me a **good** and not a **great**?" Star rubbed at her head, as if the thought was already giving her pain.

That stopped Finn in his tracks. Star stopped a second later. She was looking at the ground.

"Oh, I didn't mean it like that," she said. "I mean, grades really do not even matter, right?" She looked up and smiled a wobbly smile.

Finn shot her a look that he hoped would make her feel horrible. She hung her head even lower, so low it looked like it would tumble to the ground. Good, Finn thought. It had worked. He liked feeling angry sometimes.

It was better than feeling hopeless.

"Sorry, Finn," she whispered.

"Sorry for what?" he mumbled. But they both knew.

They walked without talking the rest of the way. They passed a few other forest houses. Most were round and covered in messy moss and vines. They were not much to look at, but Finn loved them. He loved the simple shapes of the fat, cozy homes. He loved the puffs of smoke that curled from the chimneys. It seemed to him that the houses in the forest knew what they were. So did the people that lived in them. They were not fancy, and they did not try to be. They were warm and welcoming. That was all that mattered.

The town was a different matter. Workers walked up and down the streets, casting scrubbing spells to keep everything clean. The windows sparkled in the sunlight. The doors were all spelled to be bright, bold colors. The houses reminded Finn of a new set of paints. They were beautiful, but so beautiful that you did not want to mess them up.

Finally they reached the school. It loomed over the main street like a fortress. When Finn first saw the huge stone building as a child he had tried to drag his mother away. It seemed so huge and dark. He was not afraid of the building anymore, but something about school still made him shiver sometimes. He always wondered what secrets lay tucked away in its rooms.

Finn saw his friend Willow flying above the crowd of elves, fairies, and dwarves outside the school. He waved goodbye to Star and ran away from her as fast as he could.

When he was at school he usually pretended he did not know her.

"Finn! Will you walk home with me later?" Star called out to him.

Finn ignored her. He felt guilty, but he pushed the feeling down. She is smart, he thought. She does not need me. She can take care of herself.

"Late, as usual," Willow said. She wagged a finger at him. "Are you planning to escape to the bathroom again today? You go more times a day than anyone I have ever met."

Willow was a fairy. Fairies were very proud of the fact that they were the only ones who could fly.

They were always showing off. Willow was floating just off the ground. Her wings beat silently.

All fairy wings were pretty, but Willow's were special. Most fairy wings had only one or two colors in them. Hers glittered in every color of the rainbow and sparkled under the morning light. Her pink hair fell in waves around her pale blue face.

Sam Granger walked up to them, grinning ear to ear. Sam was a dwarf girl in their class. She had big, red cheeks like apples and curly brown hair that fell to her knees. She was tall for a dwarf their age, but her head still did not reach Finn's chin. Sam was always happy and cheerful, but today her smile could have lit up the sun. Before Finn could ask why, Willow yelled, "What a beautiful dress, Sam!"

The red in Sam's cheeks now covered her whole face. Somehow her smile grew even bigger.

Of course, Finn thought. He should have noticed right away. Sam only had five dresses, one for each school day during the week.

Once when Finn was sitting behind Sam he saw that there were many places where someone had carefully mended holes. Her mother, Finn guessed. She worked as a cleaning lady in some of the rich houses in town. Sam's father had died during the Goblin Wars years ago, just like Finn's father. His mother said they had been friends, so Finn always tried to be extra nice to Sam. The dress was covered in blue flowers. Someone had spelled them to wave like a wind was blowing.

"Thank you!" Sam said. "My mother gave it to me yesterday."

Willow nodded. "I love it, Sam. It makes me think of a spring day, don't you think, Finn?"

Finn did not care much about any dress, but to be nice he said, "Definitely."

Just then Yuwen Tray and some of the town kids came slinking over. They were all looking at each other, making faces and laughing. Yuwen's hair was short and never grew. His nose was very large and pointed. When he smiled his mouth twisted into a strange, sickly shape. He had goblin blood in his family, on his father's side.

Everyone said that was why the Tray men were so mean.

"That **is** a nice dress, Sam," Yuwen said. "I think I have seen it before somewhere. Now where have I seen it...?" Yuwen made a big show of pretending to think it over.

"I know!" he said, while walking over to Sam. He pointed to a big pocket that hung at the bottom of Sam's dress. "I think I see something written on the inside of that pocket. Look inside."

Confused, Sam put her fingers inside the pocket. Finn could see small yellow letters there, but they were too small to read.

"It is three letters," Sam said. "AET." Suddenly, Sam ripped her hand away. Yuwen and his friends began to howl with laughter. Sam's eyes filled with tears and she ran into the school.

"What just happened?!" Willow shouted at Yuwen. Yuwen was grabbing at his sides, trying to catch his breath in between laughs.

"What just happened is that her dress has my sister's name inside. AET stands for Aliss Emma Tray, but I guess she didn't know that," Yuwen said. "She is wearing a dress my sister threw away."

For a moment Finn did not understand, then he put it all together - Sam's mother cleaned Yuwen's house. Yuwen's mother must have given her the dress for Sam.

Finn's mouth fell open. Usually he stayed away from Yuwen, but without thinking, he got right into Yuwen's face. He shouted, "That was horrible, Yuwen! Even for you!"

"How could you, Yuwen?" Willow yelled. "Sam has never done anything to you."

Yuwen shrugged, but still smiled. "It was just a little joke."

"Let's go, Willow," Finn said. "We still have time to find Sam before the bell."

Yuwen sneered, "She's probably in the bathroom, Finn. You were on your way there anyway, right? Just stay there with her and skip the test today. We all know you are going to fail

anyway. My dad doesn't understand why the

teachers let you come to school. It's a waste of

everyone's time."

"Shut up, Yuwen!" yelled Willow. She had

floated face to face with him. "You have failed tests.

You don't have any room to talk."

"Who cares about stupid healing spells? We have doctors for that." Yuwen's gang chuckled and followed him as he walked away.

Finn bit his bottom lip, trying to hold back the tears that wanted to roll down his cheeks. The worst part was that Yuwen was right. He **had** planned to hide in the bathroom again, just like he had said. Finn wished he could quit school, before he embarrassed himself any more.

# ◀ Chapter 3 ▶

Finn walked into the classroom and sat low in his desk chair. Willow leaned over and whispered, "Don't let that bully bother you. He's just a horrible person who wants everyone else to feel horrible, too."

Finn did not say anything. He was just too tired to respond. He was tired of Yuwen, he was tired of being Star's brother, and he was tired of tests. Most of all, he was just tired of being himself.

He wished he could trade places with someone, anyone. It would be so much easier to be someone else for a while.

Miss Dawn, his teacher, got up from her desk. "Willow, quiet please," she said. Willow's blue face turned red. "Class, today we have a test on the fire spell we have been practicing. Who would like to begin?" Many hands shot up in the air. Some children shouted, "Me! Me!" Miss Dawn put a finger to her lips. "Quiet, please. One at a time."

She called on a boy dwarf. He stood and put his hands in front of his face. His lips moved as he softly repeated the spell they had learned. Suddenly a small orange fire flickered over his hands. He opened his eyes and smiled when he saw the flames. Miss Dawn nodded. "Well done, Silas," she said. "You may sit down."

One by one, other children stood up and tried to cast the fire spell. Almost every one passed. Children who failed could practice at home and then try again later. Finn never tried again. There was never any point.

He looked around the classroom. Only a few children were left waiting to take the test. It was now or never. He slipped his body out of his desk and tiptoed away. Then he heard Yuwen's voice yelling from the back of the room.

"Miss Dawn, There he goes again! Are you going to set fire to the bathroom, Finn?"

Finn froze. Several children giggled. Finn looked back at Yuwen's sneering face and cold smile. Suddenly anger swelled in his stomach.

Finn heard Miss Dawn's voice telling him to sit down, but he was not listening. He was thinking only of the fire spell. Usually the words got mixed up in his mind, but today they were clear. They seemed to come alive, moving and swirling inside him.

Finn stretched out his hands and summoned the fire. Electricity shot into Finn's legs and out through his arms. In his mind's eye he saw a clear image of a blazing blue fire, with flames so tall they licked the ceiling.

Suddenly he heard screams around him. He looked up. He was frightened by what he saw: one side of his classroom was on fire! The big blue flames from his mind were rushing up, up, to the ceiling. They were burning up everything in their path. He backed away from the blaze.

A hand pressed on his shoulder.

"End the spell, Finn. You must end the spell." Miss Dawn whispered. Somehow, she sounded calm.

At first Finn could not move his arms or legs, even though he wanted to. They were frozen in place. Around him the yelling grew more frantic. Then he looked up at Miss Dawn's clear gray eyes.

"End the spell, Finn," she repeated. He willed his arms to reach out in front of him. For the first time in his life he had to finish a spell. In his mind he pictured the fire shrinking into nothingness. Instantly the fire vanished, but it had done its work. The stone wall now looked dirty and black. The paintings and drawings that had hung there fell to ash on the ground.

Finn's classmates were staring at him in shock. Yuwen's mouth hung open. Most of the children just looked confused.

Finn did not know what to do, so he just sat down. He tried not to look at all the eyes that were fixed on him.

An instant later the room exploded with loud applause.

One by one, every child but Yuwen stood up and started clapping and cheering loudly for Finn. Miss Dawn clapped the loudest of all, but she was not smiling like the children. With her eyes still on Finn, she said in a distracted voice, "Class, it is now Free Time. Have a good afternoon. Those of you who have not taken the test may do so tomorrow. Finn, I would like to talk to you. Please come to my desk for a moment."

Fairies, dwarves, and elves leapt out of their chairs and ran or flew from the classroom. Finn stayed in his chair. He looked longingly at the door.

She must be so angry, he thought. And she is right to be. My fire could have gotten out of control. I will always lose Free Time no matter what I do!

Suddenly Finn felt something hard shove him in the ribs. He yelped in pain. He spun his head just in time to see Yuwen disappear into the hallway.

# ◀ Chapter 4 ▶

Finn rubbed his head, which was now throbbing. Miss Dawn looked like she was herself again. She poured herself a cup of tea. Finn wondered what his punishment would be for the fire. Magical mishaps sometimes happened, and as long as no one got hurt the teachers were not usually harsh.

He checked the blackened back wall of the classroom. No one had been hurt, but the wall was ruined. Even worse, he had put people in danger. A sick feeling rose up in Finn as he thought of the punishment he would get.

Miss Dawn set the tea down. "Would you like a cup?" she asked. Finn shook his head. He wished she would just get on with whatever she wanted to say.

Miss Dawn was part elf and part fairy, but she looked more like an elf. She did not have wings, but her skin was the leafiest green you could imagine. Her eyes were the deep gray of storm clouds. Right now they were locked on Finn's face. She did not look angry, though. She looked extremely interested...in Finn.

"That was very well done, Finn," she said. "The size of the fire and its blue color were amazing. I have never actually seen anyone do that before." Finally she broke her stare and took a sip from her mug.

Finn bit down on his lip. He hated this waiting. He wished Miss Dawn would just get to the point and give him his punishment.

"Finn," she said. "What you did was very....odd. You did not really know what you were doing, did you?" she asked. Finn shook his head. It had been a shock to him, too.

Miss Dawn nodded. "That's what I thought."

"Am I in trouble?" Finn asked.

Miss Dawn took a deep breath. "No, Finn. I'm not angry, but I do need something from you. I need to know if you can cast that spell again." She set the cup on the table and looked at him. "Please try. Try to cast the fire in the same spot, along the wall."

"But the burned wall-" he began.

"This is more important."

Finn took a deep breath and put his hands out in front of him. He began to say the words of the spell, over and over. They got a little mixed up in his mind, but he kept repeating them. He opened his eyes. There was nothing in the air in front of him.

Finn clenched his fists and shut his eyes tightly. Before he could try again, Miss Dawn stopped him.

"No, Finn. It's alright." Then she tapped at her mouth with a finger. "Finn, I have good news and bad news. Which would you like to hear first?"

Finn looked at the clock. Free Time was almost over!

"It doesn't matter," he said.

She leaned over her desk so that she was very close to him. "The good news is that you have talent. You know that your great grandfather was extremely talented. He was famous for his skill. Strong magic runs in your family."

Finn knew all this. He knew that he was the only slow one in his entire family. He knew it better than anyone. Why was his teacher rubbing it in?

Miss Dawn looked at him and the gray in her eyes darkened. "Finn, you have it, too. I promise you that. But you may learn magic a little differently than others. I think that I can help you, if you will let me. I would like us to work together before school each day. I think that if you really try, we can have you ready for the Magic Games next month."

# ◀ Chapter 5 ▶

Finn's jaw dropped. Had Miss Dawn gone completely crazy?

"The Magic Games? But Miss Dawn, only two children from every class go to the Games. The best two children in magic! Right now I'm the **worst** in the entire school. There's no way that I can catch up to everyone by then! Besides, all of my teachers have tried to help me before. It has never worked, not even a little."

During his second year in magic school he was given extra homework, and during his third year his teacher had always punished him. She told him he was just lazy.

"I know, Finn," she said. "And I am sure that they were all good teachers doing their best, but they did not see what I just saw."

Finn was confused. "What did you see?"

Miss Dawn pulled an old, dusty magic book from a drawer and set it on her desk. It had colorful bookmarks all over its pages. She flipped through the pages and then put her finger on a sentence. "Read this, please."

**Makers lived long ago in our world. They could change spells as they wished. In fact, they could create new spells. They used their gifts and**

wrote down their spells for others to study. No one knows why, but Maker children stopped being born. Over time, all the Makers vanished. However, they created all the spells we cast today. That was their gift to us.

Finn looked up at Miss Dawn. What did any of this have to do with him?

"Finn," Miss Dawn began. "All the magic that we teach is magic that the Makers created. We can copy it and practice it, but none of us can **change** it."

She sounded a little sad.

"But those are the rules," Finn replied. "The Makers are all gone. They gave us all the magic there was. That is how things work." He started tapping his foot. All of a sudden he did not like where this talk was going.

Miss Dawn stared at him without blinking. Her gray eyes began to swirl with other colors, greens and blues. It scared him a little, but he could not look away.

"But what if the Makers are coming back?" she whispered. "Finn, I think that may be what is happening – and I think **you** may be one of them." She rested her hand on his.

Finn pulled his hand away. He wanted to run. This was all too much. He did not want any of it. He did not want to stay in for Free Time. He did not want to be having a strange talk with his teacher. And he definitely did not want to be a Maker, or anything else that would make him feel any more of a misfit than he already was.

"Miss Dawn, I'm not a Maker. I have only done one spell correctly in all the years I have been at school. Makers were smart. We both know that I am stupid."

Miss Dawn shook her head sternly. "Finn, you are NOT stupid, and I do not want you saying that ever again. Your mind just sees things in a different way. Magic has been hard for you because Makers are not good at casting a spell in the same way over and over. To cast magic, they need to change spells. But you have to see that for yourself.

Tonight I want you to go back over your spell book. Find a spell that you have been wanting to cast, and play around with it. Picture it in your mind and let it take on a life of its own. See what happens, okay? **But don't use a fire spell. Try**

**something else."** Then she closed the book with a **clap**.

Finn knew that it was better to say nothing, so he nodded and jogged outside. Miss Dawn had to be wrong, of course. But her words had dug their way into his head and now he could not get them out. Deep inside of himself he heard a whisper. It spoke in a tiny little voice, nagging at him.

**What if it is true?**

# ◀ Chapter 6 ▶

The Forest of Burns was the same color as
the wall Finn had destroyed - black. Some of the
worst battles of the Goblin Wars had been fought
there. The trees that were left looked sad, their bark
covered with ash. People had cast planting and
growing spells here. Others had tried gardening
without any magic at all, but the forest was too
stubborn. Nothing grew.

Children were sitting on stumps around small pits, practicing their fire magic. Some of the lazier students were toasting marshmallows. As soon as Finn walked near the pits, he heard whispers. Willow jumped up and ran toward him. Her body just missed one student's blast of red hot flame.

"Finn, how did you do it?!" she cried. "That spell is supposed to make a **small** fire, not some huge one! Where did you find that other spell? And why didn't you tell me you were going to do that?"

Finn shrugged. "I dunno."

Willow narrowed her eyes, so he added, "I have only ever tried the spell twice and it didn't work. I was about to go hide in the bathroom, but then I got angry. I guess I wanted it to work so badly that it really did."

Willow's blue hands were on her hips. "But how did you get such a massive fire, Finn? The spell makes a tiny one!"

Finn shook his head. "I don't know. I was so angry I don't remember doing it. I swear that is the truth. I don't understand it any more than you do."

Willow frowned. "Okay, I believe you. But now it's a real mystery. You must have learned some other fire spell. What did Miss Dawn say about it?"

Finn did not want to talk about Miss Dawn's crazy ideas, so he told part of the truth. "Something about me learning differently and more homework."

A voice behind him called his name. Finn looked back to see Star running toward them. A bag of books that was almost as big as she was banged against her short legs with each step.

"Finn! Why did you start walking without me? You know Mother says you need to wait for me!" she yelled. Finn looked at Willow, then rolled his eyes as Star reached them.

"Why do you always follow me around?" he demanded. "It's embarrassing ."

"You really should be nicer to her, Finn!" Willow snapped. "She looks up to you. You are so lucky to have a sister." Finn did not respond. Willow did not have any sisters or brothers, so she did not know how annoying they could be.

Star looked tired from running with all of her books.

"Everyone....is....talking....about....your...spell!" she panted.

Finn shrugged. "Star, I don't want to talk about it, okay? I don't know how I did it. I will probably never be able to cast a spell again. End of story."

"But-" she began.

He cut her off. "That's all I know, Star! Now stop bothering me and go away."

First Star looked surprised, then tears welled up in her eyes. She turned and ran, her huge bag thumping behind her. Willow called after her, but Star kept running.

Willow glared at Finn. "That was not very nice,

Finn. Why do you always take things out on her?

She was just happy for you."

Finn kicked at a rock. "I need to get home.

See you tomorrow, Willow." He turned and marched

into the forest.

# ◀ Chapter 7 ▶

Finn softly opened the back door of his house. Could he enter without anyone spotting him? He peeked inside. The back room was empty. He pushed the door shut as gently as he could. It scraped against the floor. Finn froze, waiting for someone to hear him. No one did, so he tiptoed down to the basement.

His great-grandfather's work desk faced the peaceful back yard. His mother's rose bushes zigzagged through the deep green grass. Finn lit a candle and touched the dark brown wood with his fingertips. The desk was one of the oldest things his family owned. His grandparents had used it, then his parents. Now only his mother did, but she said that one day Finn would, too.

It made him feel powerful to sit in the same chair that his family had used. It also made him feel loved. His mother often told him that they were still watching over him. Sometimes he thought he could feel them there.

"Find a spell..." Miss Dawn had said. "A spell you want to try, and let your mind **change** it." He pulled the heavy magic book from his bag and threw it on the desk with a **thud.** He flipped through the pages, looking for a spell that called to him.

Finn still did not believe that he was a Maker. First of all, all of the Makers had vanished long ago. Also, a Maker would be someone who was good at magic, someone who thought it was easy. That was definitely **not** him. After all, the fire spell was the first spell he had ever cast in his whole life. Star had cast two spells on her first day of magic school, when she was **six**.

Finn kept flipping through the book, not finding anything that looked interesting. Then a spell popped out at him. It read:

**Floating Spell**

**This spell will allow you to float and glide over the ground.**

He had always wanted to float like Willow. Sometimes he even had dreams that he was flying. In the dreams it always felt wonderful to soar into the air with the birds. A flying spell would be even more fun, he thought. But everyone knew that there **were** no flying spells.

Well, floating is better than being stuck on the ground, Finn thought to himself. So he decided to give it a try. He read the words out loud, then closed his eyes and repeated them in his mind. Nothing happened. "I knew it," he said to the empty room. He was about to close the book, but then he remembered what Miss Dawn had told him to do. He relaxed his mind.

"Okay, brain," he said. "I really want to do this. Show me what to say. I promise to listen." Finn felt a little silly talking to his brain, but he did not know what else to do. He waited. Colors began to swirl in

his mind. Then pictures came, and finally the words

of a very powerful spell that Finn could not control.

# ◀ Chapter 8 ▶

**Bang!** Finn was suddenly thrown into the air. His head hit something hard. He opened his eyes and saw that he was pressed against a wall.

What kind of spell makes you stick to a wall? he wondered. He turned his head to look around.

His insides did a flip when he realized what had happened. He was not on a wall at all! He was stuck to the ceiling! And he was not stuck, not really. His body just wanted to get as high as it could, so it had taken him to the ceiling. I'm a lot higher than I should be for a floating spell, he thought. I wonder how high I could go?

He needed to get outside so that he could test it. But how to get down? He relaxed his mind again but kept his eyes open. "Lower me to the floor," he said out loud. Right away he sunk down so that he floated over the floor.

"Move me to the door," he commanded. He opened the door. It was getting easier now.

Then he tried just **thinking** what he wanted without saying it out loud. I want to go to the back door, he thought. His body did it! He grabbed the door and pushed it open. The cool night air felt wonderful on his face.

This is so great! he thought, looking down at the ground below him. It was time to see what the spell could really do. His body sped into the air, soaring up, up, up. Soon he was as high as the tallest trees. He pressed his arms flat against his body. The wind slapped at his face and eyes, but he did not care. Soon he was zipping through the trees and looking down on the houses below.

"This is so cool!" he yelled, and a group of nearby birds honked in return. Then he saw Star, far below. She was sitting on a tree trunk, her head in her hands, curled up into a ball. She rocked back and forth in a strange way. If he didn't know better, he would have thought she was crying bitterly. But Star never cried. She was too perfect.

Still, something was wrong with her.

Finn flew around for a while, wondering if he should say something to Star, but nothing came to him. She would get over it soon. Maybe she would finally understand that at school she needed to take care of herself.

Finn saw that it was getting dark. His family might be worried that he had not returned home yet. He changed direction and zoomed back toward home. Star was no longer sitting alone on the tree trunk.

He wanted to tell his family about the spell. His aunt had read just about every history book ever published, and his uncle had been to the faraway lands in the Goblin Wars. They would know whether or not he was a Maker. Finn really hoped not. Mother had told him that Makers got into horrible accidents. She said the spells they invented did not always turn out like they hoped. This made Finn

shiver.

# ◀ Chapter 9 ▶

Lower me down to the ground, Finn thought as he came closer to his house. He felt himself falling, and finally landed on the soft grass. He pictured the spell slipping out of his hands back into the forest. In a few moments he knew he had ended the spell. He could not believe this was the second spell he had ended in just one day. None of it felt real.

Finn looked at his house, the house he had lived in his whole life. In many ways, it looked the same as it always did. Its round wooden walls were light brown and dotted with seven small arched windows. Smoke puffed out of the curling brick chimney. Finn rubbed at his arms. He had been so excited by his flying spell that he had not noticed the cold night air.

Finn slipped inside the half-moon front door on tiptoes. His whole family was sitting at the kitchen table, looking very cross.

His mother seemed especially angry. She was sitting with her arms tightly folded. His aunt and uncle were seated next to Star, his aunt holding her close. Star's eyes were puffy.

Finn took a deep breath. "I'm sorry I'm late," he said. Star began to sniffle. "And I'm sorry I was mean to Star. I won't be that way again."

Star sniffled again and hung her head.

His mother pointed to a chair. He slunk down into it. Her eyes were flashing and her hair was standing on end. "Do you have any idea how worried we were? Going out at night by yourself! Trying out strange new fire spells! Disappearing into the forest, when it's dangerous!"

Finn hung his head. He hated to make his mother upset. She worked so hard and did so much for him. It made him feel sick inside when he let her down. He needed to tell her, to explain everything. Then she would understand. They all would. Maybe they could help him.

"I had to test something that my teacher told me..."

Finn told his family about the blue fire and his talk with Miss Dawn. Then he explained how he had somehow changed a floating spell into a flying spell.

His family members' eyes grew wider and wider as they listened to his tale. When he had finished, his aunt was staring at Finn strangely, like he had some kind of illness. His uncle looked as if he was thinking everything over. His mother just seemed confused.

"I don't understand, Finn," she said finally. "Is this a joke? All the Makers are gone. It has been many, many years since any of them have lived. What you are saying is impossible."

Finn shook his head. "I promise you I'm not joking, Mother," he said. "I don't understand it, either."

There was a long silence.

His uncle rubbed his hands together, grinning with excitement. "Well, Finn, I would very much like to see this flying spell. I have never heard of a flying spell before, not a true one. May we see it?"

Finn nodded. "Let's go outside and I will show you!"

"Wait a minute!" His aunt interrupted. "It's getting dark. What if Finn crashes into a tree branch or hurts himself?"

Finn's mother spoke in a soft voice. "It's all right. I think I remember a spell for that." She turned to Finn. "I don't know what to think about all of this, Finn. But I do know that you almost never lie."

"I don't plan to start now," Finn said, his face feeling suddenly very hot. "Maybe I am crazy, but I am not a liar." Then he jumped up and bolted out the door, with the rest of his family following behind.

# ◀ Chapter 10 ▶

They gathered in a small group in the yard. Finn's mother closed her eyes and silently chanted the words of the spell. Tiny lights appeared all around them, dancing in the air. They hung like candles, some just above their heads. Others rose high into the treetops, casting everything in a warm glow. Each of Finn's family members turned to him, waiting.

Finn's insides were doing flips and his hands were shaking. **Please let me be able to do this**, he thought. **Please, please**. He closed his eyes and tried his best to let his mind go blank. He let the words from the floating spell begin to swirl in his mind. Time seemed to move very slowly. Then, after what seemed like forever, he felt himself being lifted slowly from the ground. He opened his eyes. His family was silent, but wide-eyed.

**Time to show them what I can do**, he thought. He looked above him to make sure his path was clear. He saw only beautiful open air, now lit by the tiny glowing lights. He knew what to do.

With a deep breath, Finn zoomed up into the sky. He heard his family gasp from below. Flying was just as wonderful as before, just as natural. He was feeling bold now, so he did a few flips in the air.

He spun and zoomed around the sky. It was not bright enough to see his family's faces from up so high, so he flew down closer to them.

What he saw made him smile. His aunt's mouth hung open in shock. His mother was crying. His uncle was grinning. His sister was jumping up and down.

This is real, Finn thought. I really did it! **And best of all, I am not crazy!**

He touched down gently and ended the spell.

In an instant they were all around him. He put out his own arms and hugged all the bodies his hands could find.

After a few moments everyone untangled themselves and began talking all at once. Star chattered about spells. Finn's aunt was asking when they should tell the Elders. His uncle was telling stories about Makers in the family long, long ago. Only his mother was silent. She just looked at him. Finally she waved her hand, silencing everyone else. Then she hunched down to Finn's level and looked Finn right in the eye.

"Finn, I'm going to pay your teacher a visit tonight." She looked around at the rest of the family. "Everyone else, please tell no one about this. Miss Dawn and I will think this over together and come up with a plan."

Everyone agreed. Finn's aunt, uncle, and Star all headed back into the house. Finn turned to leave as well, but his mother caught his hands and held them tightly in hers. "Finn, my son, I'm very proud of you, and very happy for you. But you need to know that everything is going to change, and not all of the changes may be good. For right now, just enjoy this moment. And Finn - wherever he is, your father is proud of you."

Finn's eyes welled with tears. He nodded and smiled. Then his mother went back inside to make hot chocolate for everyone.

As Finn followed her, he wondered if his life could get any stranger.

# ◄ Chapter 11 ►

Mother woke Finn early the next morning. Her warm hand rubbed his arm, pulling him out of a dream. In the dream he was being chased by a horrible goblin. He bolted up, still thinking it was really happening. Then he saw his mother and relaxed.

"Bad dream?" she asked. He nodded.

"I'm sorry about waking you so early, but this is how it's going to be from now on. You will get used to it after a few days."

"Why?" he asked, confused.

"I spoke to your teacher last night," she said. "We think the best thing to do is have you compete in the Games." Mother's voice sounded unsure, almost worried. Maybe she thought he would not do well at the Games? He understood how she felt. "Mother, there is no way that I-" Finn began.

She interrupted him, her face set in a stern line. "Finn, you will do just fine. I am not worried about that at all. From now on you will go to school early. Miss Dawn has agreed to tutor you."

"Not another tutor!" he yelled, throwing his body back on the bed. He grabbed a pillow and hid his face.

His mother sighed. "Finn, now that we know how your magic works, I promise you that things will get much, much easier. You just learn a little differently than some children..."

Finn interrupted her, "Yeah, like Star the perfect student..."

Mother gave him an even sterner look. "**Everyone** learns differently from one another," she said. "Every single one. Sports and building things have always been easy for you, but they are hard for Star. Yes, Star has an easy time reading spells, but you have your own talents."

His mother dropped her voice to a whisper and leaned in closer to him. "You are a Maker, Finn. I don't know how. I don't know why. But I know what you are. This is..." she began. "This is something none of us really understand yet. So for right now, I need you to promise me you will tell no one. Do you understand? Not even Willow."

Finn nodded, confused and scared.

"Oh, and one more thing," she said. "Until the Games, don't change or make any new spells unless you are alone with Miss Dawn. Do you understand? In school, just try to read them as they are, even if that means you can't cast them. Okay?"

Finn nodded again. His mother had been gripping his arm tightly. Now she looked down at her hand and let him go. She patted his knee once. Then she left to make breakfast, leaving Finn feeling very much alone.

# ◀ Chapter 12 ▶

Finn had thought that he would be walking to school by himself, but Star was waiting for him downstairs. She did not seem to mind leaving early at all.

"Mom says that I get to stay with you and your teacher until the morning bell," she told him happily. "Your teacher said it was okay!" Star was hopping next to him to keep up. Her huge bag of books jiggled with each step.

Oh great, thought Finn. I even get to have Star the star with me during my tutoring session. Just what I want - help from my little sister. As usual, Star did not seem to have any idea how Finn felt. She just babbled on about how nice Miss Dawn was and how she could not wait to be in her class.

When they walked into the classroom, Miss Dawn was waiting for them. She had books and spell sheets spread out on the table. She greeted Star warmly.

"Star, I'm glad you will be coming to our meetings. I have heard so many wonderful things about you," Miss Dawn said.

Star looked like she was about to float away without any magic at all. She had a huge, silly smile on her face. Her cheeks and the tips of her pointed ears had turned bright pink.

"Do you mind working on your own school work quietly while Finn and I practice?"

"Yes! Sure! I will work over here!" Star's words tumbled out of her. She pulled a textbook out of her giant bag and began to read.

Finn turned to his teacher, suddenly feeling the need to escape.

"Can I go to the-" Finn began.

Miss Dawn crossed her arms. "No, Finn, you may not use the bathroom unless it is really an emergency, and I do not think it is." Now it was Finn's turn to blush. "Please come and sit down so that we can begin."

For the next hour Finn worked harder than he had ever worked in school before. Miss Dawn had spent the whole night reading about Makers and how they learned. She said that their brains worked a little differently than everyone else's. It was harder for them to read spells that were already written, but they were really good at thinking up new ways to do things. She kept using the word **creative**. Makers were creative.

Finn asked her why it took him so long to gain his powers, but Miss Dawn said that she did not know. The Makers had kept many secrets about how their magic worked. People knew very little about them, just stories that people had told over the years.

Finn had hoped that during his tutoring he would just get to make up his own spells, but Miss Dawn said no. She told him that he needed to learn to cast the old ones **and** to make new ones. She said his brain was jumping all over the place. It had to learn to slow down. It had to learn **control**.

So they practiced.

They practiced with spell cards and books. They practiced reading spells and writing spells and seeing them in Finn's mind. The most fun part was when Miss Dawn let him create a new spell, but then she made him practice doing **that** the same way over and over.

Boring!

There were times when Finn got frustrated - **very** frustrated. Sometimes he wanted to throw the book across the room. But Miss Dawn always helped him to calm down. She told him that he had to start being more kind and understanding with himself. When he got really upset, she told him jokes. They were terrible jokes.

"What did the sea say to the mermaid?" she asked him. "Nothing! It just waved."

Finn would always groan at these jokes, but in the end they always laughed together at how bad they were.

Miss Dawn was kind of strange, but Finn liked her. He liked how he felt about himself when he was around her. She believed in him. Because of this, he was starting to believe in himself too.

# ◀ Chapter 13 ▶

The next month Finn worked nonstop. It turned out being a Maker was a full-time job. Miss Dawn gave him extra homework every night, and then every morning they worked together before school. He was so tired he could not keep his eyes open in his daytime classes.

But he was making a lot of progress.

He could finally cast some spells from his book: Ice spells, shrinking spells, mending spells.

Many of them were still too hard for him, but Miss Dawn told him that someday he would be able to cast any one he wanted. She said that it might just take time.

Finn's real power was in thinking up new spells. That was the fun part. It felt like building towns with blocks when he was little. Now he stacked pictures and words in his mind. He thought of one little piece, and then he added to that. He kept adding until he had that feeling that told him the spell was done.

Miss Dawn had asked him how he knew when a new spell was ready, but he could not really explain it. How do you know when a picture you paint is finished? You just know, deep inside.

Finally, the morning of the Games arrived. All of the classes were walking in lines to the Magic

Field, chattering about who they thought would win. Children always tried to guess who would be competing. Most of the time it was easy to figure out. Star, for example, had been picked every year.

In fact, almost everyone in the school had guessed each pair of children who were competing this year... all except one. In Finn's class, Yuwen had been chosen. Even though he was not supposed to tell, he had bragged about it to anyone who would listen. But even Yuwen did not know who the other person from the class would be. Children had been asking and pointing fingers at one another for days. "Is it you?" they asked their friends suspiciously.

For weeks, Finn had been feeling nervous that he would have to lie if someone asked him. After all, he had promised his mother that he would not tell.

But no one asked, not even Willow. They talked to him about it and wondered who he thought it might be, of course. They just never believed it could be him.

Finn thought it was funny, but also a little frustrating. He had been doing so much better in school, but they still saw him as the Old Finn, not the New Finn. If he did not feel so sick, he might enjoy seeing the shock on their faces when the teachers called his name.

# ◀ Chapter 14 ▶

Finn sat with his class on the edge of the field. He wished that he had thrown up before his class left the school. Now it was too late.

He was looking at this year's magical obstacle course. Each year the teachers picked the partners out of a hat, so sometimes the partners were fair and sometimes they were not. Last year Star had been partnered with another girl her age from Year 1. They had played against many teams of older children. But that was just part of the Games. Each team got two scores at the end. One was for how fast they moved through the course, and the other was for how well they worked together. So it was not just about speed.

Every year the course changed, but there were always three big obstacles. Only magic could be used. Anyone in Year 3 or older had to use a different spell for each task. Finn looked closely at the field. He saw a deep pit, a large pond, and a high wooden wall. With the pit he could use the floating spell he had worked on. With the wall he could use his flying spell. Finn guessed he could try an ice spell on the pond, but his ice spells did not always work. **Please let me get a good partner**, he begged silently.

Principal Elora was seated on a chair that floated into the middle of the Field. She was wrinkled and her hair was stark white, but she always spoke in a clear voice. It sounded like the voice of a much younger person somehow. But Principal Elora was definitely not young. She had been the principal even when his parents had been in school. "Welcome, everyone, to the Magic Games!"

Everyone cheered and clapped loudly. She raised a hand and the crowd grew silent. "I will now announce the teams. When you hear your name, please take your place at the starting line with your partner."

She began to read the names of the partner groups. Children walked two by two onto the field.

Yuwen got partnered with a Year 8 fairy named Gregory. He was older and bigger than Yuwen but looked just as mean.

Those two will be perfect for each other, Finn thought. They might actually win, or they might just end up hitting each other in the dirt. That would be pretty fun to watch.

Then Miss Dawn read, "Star Millay and Finn Millay." Finn's mouth hung open. All of his classmates turned and stared at him. They began to whisper and shout questions. He heard Willow screech, "Why didn't you TELL ME?!"

He ignored all of it. All he could do was order his feet to move forward and bring him to his partner... who just happened to be his little sister.

# ◀ Chapter 15 ▶

Finn walked to the field and took his place

next to Star. She looked just as shocked as he was.

She looked nervous too. He wondered why, since

she had done well at the Games last year. Her team

had won third place.

Star had been watching Finn's tutoring work

with Miss Dawn, so she knew that his magic had

gotten much better. But she also knew that he had

good days and bad days. Sometimes he could do spells without a problem, but at other times it was still hard. Oh no, he realized. I **did** get a better partner! Star is going to do all the magic, and I'll be made fun of forever! He could just hear Yuwen sneering, "Finn, thank goodness you had your little sister with you. Your little sister saves you from everything." A bad taste rose up in Finn's throat.

He tried to calm himself while the other partners took their turns on the field. Star leaned over to him.

She whispered, "I was thinking about an ice spell for the pond. You can do that, right? And then what about a jumping spell for the pit, okay?"

Finn bit down on his lip. He could do the ice spell, where every step you took froze the water, but he had never been able to make his jumping spell work.

"Could we do a floating spell for the pit?" he asked. If your partner could do a spell and you could not, you could hold onto them. Older kids usually did this with younger kids. Sometimes they actually scooped the little kids up in their arms. Everyone thought it was cute, since the little kids did not usually know many spells.

But this was different. Most little kids were not like Star. And Finn was the older brother. He did not want to be holding onto Star as she did her magic. He would look silly and stupid. I never should have agreed to this, he thought to himself. This was the biggest mistake of my life.

By now, six of the teams had already finished the course. Yuwen and Gregory had the best time so far, but they had lost points for teamwork. They had not hit each other, but they had gotten close. It was almost Finn and Star's turn.

Star had agreed to use the ice spell. "But if you can't get yours to work quickly, you have to hold onto me, Finn!" she said. "Promise? It will look just as silly if we are stuck at the pond."

Finn nodded. She was right. And they did need to move quickly.

"But for the wall, I'm using my flying spell, okay? Miss Dawn said I have to use one of my Maker spells today. It's the perfect task for it."

She smiled. "Sure, Finn. I'd love to fly with you."

Finn looked at her, He had never realized it before, but with her smile and her curly, crazy hair, she looked a lot like their father. His hair had been a mess of curls, too. She had his same smile, the same pale skin, and the same big green eyes.

Suddenly Finn felt badly about how he had been treating Star. He had not been a very good brother to her. Actually, he had been a terrible one. All this time, he had been angry at her just because he had trouble with magic. It was like he thought she had taken it from him, as if it were all her fault.

He thought about how she still loved him. She had always believed in him. He saw a picture of them in his mind as grown ups. If he did not change, would she still feel that way in ten years or twenty? Probably not, he thought. They would not be close anymore, not feel like family. She deserved better. She deserved a brother who took care of her and looked out for her, just like she did for him. Just like their father would have done for both of them.

# ◀ Chapter 16 ▶

Miss Dawn called their names. Finn took

Star's hand in his. She looked surprised. He tried to

smile at her, but he was so nervous that it came out

lopsided. She smiled back. We can do this, he

thought. Around them the crowd was cheering

loudly. They seemed to love that there was a

brother and sister team.

They took their places at the starting line and waited. The deep hole was about ten feet in front of them. Finn was already practicing the floating spell in his mind. Then a loud bang rang through the air, announcing they could start.

Finn and Star began chanting the floating spell as fast as they could. Finn's eyes were shut tightly and his hands were clenched in fists. He wanted nothing in the world as badly as he wanted this spell to work. **Almost there**, he thought. **Almost there**...

He felt his body lifting off the ground. Yes! He had done it. Star had already gotten her spell to work, and she was waiting for him. Finn put out his hand, and she took it. They floated quickly over the pit, then both finished the spell in their minds.

The pond was next. Finn closed his eyes and repeated the ice spell over and over, but something was wrong. The words kept getting mixed up in his mind. He started to get frustrated and angry, which made everything worse. He could hear the crowd whispering around them.

"Change of plans, Finn!" Star called out. "The ice spell doesn't work well for two. We are about to take one giant jump!" She grabbed his arm tightly in hers, and before Finn knew what had happened, he was being lifted into the air. She was pulling him with her, but he could feel himself slipping. She grabbed his other arm and they held each other in a tight hug. Then he felt himself falling and they were back on solid ground.

The crowd went wild, cheering and clapping. The audience loved it. Finn knew that everyone had seen what had happened, that Star had been the one who cast the spell. But you know what? That's okay, he thought. I'm proud of her.

He turned to her and grinned. "Thanks, Star. You saved us back there."

She blushed, looking as happy as he had ever seen her. In that moment nothing else mattered. Not who won the contest, not what their scores were, not what anyone said. None of it made any difference.

"You ready to fly?" he asked her.

She nodded. "Show them what you can do, Finn!"

Finn bent down and Star hopped on his back. She put her hands around his neck and held on. Finn let his mind go blank and allowed the flying spell to come to him. He had done it so many times before that it came easily, like an old friend. He repeated the spell over and over, and felt them both being lifted off the ground.

The crowd became louder. Finn heard parts of their words. "Floating spell..." they were saying. "That won't work with that high wall!" Others scolded, "But they already used that one!"

Finn laughed and yelled out, "This isn't any floating spell! Watch this!" Then he zoomed up, into the air, flying higher than the wall. Star let out a happy shout, then they zoomed down to the ground

again, banking and landing right at the finish line.
Star hopped down, giggling.

Finn looked at the crowd. It was now
completely hushed. Everyone was staring at him.
Many of them were pointing and whispering. He
suddenly wondered if using one of his Maker spells
had been a bad idea. The faces around him did not
look happy or even impressed. They looked
confused and frightened. Star huddled closer to
him, looking just as scared as he felt.

# ◀ Chapter 17 ▶

Finn and Star had been the last team to compete. They had gotten the third fastest time. All they had to do now was to wait while the judges talked and added up everyone's scores. All of the children who had competed were sitting together on a bench. Everyone except Yuwen was asking Finn a hundred questions about his flying spell. They were talking and shouting over each other. Finn was trying to answer as many questions as he could, but he had to yell over all the noise.

"How did you do it?" one asked. "Where did you find that spell?"

All of them agreed that they had never heard of a flying spell before. "Did you discover a secret book of spells?" another wondered. "Did you tell the teachers?"

Finn's head was beginning to hurt. Luckily Miss Dawn rescued him. She gathered Finn in her arms and squeezed him tightly. Finn hugged her back, even though it was embarrassing. She whispered, "Well done, Finn." She gripped his shoulders and stared into his eyes one last time. Then she smiled and walked away.

Finn took his seat again just as Principal Elora's floating chair took its place in the middle of the Field. She waved a hand, and the crowd grew silent. It was time to call up the winners.

She began to read the top scores. Two of the younger dwarf boys had done very well. They had placed fourth. Third place went to a Year 5 elf girl and a Year 6 dwarf girl. Finn and Star looked at one another. They had been hoping for third or fourth place. Now they probably would not get a prize at all. Oh well, thought Finn. At least I got the flying spell to work. Star frowned.

"Don't worry about it, Star," Finn whispered. "You did great. I'm proud that you were my partner."

Star stared at the ground, looking pleased and embarrassed at the same time. "You were great, too, Finn," she croaked.

Principal Elora's voice rang out. "And now we would like to announce the second place team. It is Yuwen from Year 5 and Gregory from Year 8. This team also earned the fastest time. Well done, boys," she said. Yuwen and Gregory stomped across the Field. They were kicking up angry clods of dirt with each step.

"They are **such** bad sports," Star whispered. Finn laughed and nodded.

Principal Elora spoke again. "Finally, I would like to announce the winning team. This team did not have the fastest time, but they worked together very well. The judges also felt that they used a lot of creativity during the race. Star and Finn Millay have been awarded first prize. Star and Finn, please come get your trophy. Congratulations!"

The crowd jumped to their feet and cheered. Star and Finn just looked at each other, stunned. They could not believe what they had heard. The other kids around them were pushing them forward.

"We did it!" Star finally yelled, leaping up. Finn followed her toward Miss Dawn. His teacher handed them a beautiful trophy. Its magical moving parts were lit from the inside by twinkling stars.

She shook each of their hands. He then thanked Principal Elora and began to walk back toward his seat, but she stopped him. "Stay here a moment," she whispered. "I hear there is one more matter at hand."

Star looked at Finn with a question in her eyes, but he shook his head. He had no idea what was happening either.

Miss Dawn floated in the center of the field. Now it was her turn to hush the crowd. "Good morning, everyone. For those of you who do not know me, my name is Kora Dawn. I have been a teacher here for over fifteen years. In that time I have been lucky enough to teach many groups of wonderful children. I thought I had seen it all, until this year when I met young Finn."

She cleared her throat. All eyes were on her. "I know that you were probably very shocked when you saw Finn fly today. Any adult knows that no spell for flying exists in any of the books. The Makers never wrote one. Well, I am here to tell you that now one has. You may not believe this, but Finn Millay is a Maker. I have been working with him for the past month, and I have seen it with my own eyes. I promise you that what I say is true. We all thought that the Makers had vanished. In fact they live again. Please meet Finn Millay, Maker and inventor of spells!"

The crowd roared, cheering and yelling and shouting questions. Finn took a step back. He had been wishing for a moment like this all of his life. Now that it was really happening, he was suddenly scared.

Principal Elora waved her hand. "Yes, I am sure that you have questions. However, we ask you to give Finn and his family time first. They will discuss all this with the Elders. You will be told when we learn more." The crowd settled a bit, satisfied with this.

"Thank you, Principal Elora," said Miss Dawn. "I for one am hopeful that Finn is just our first discovery. Finn's powers mean that the Makers are returning, to help and guide us once more!"

Everyone cheered loudly again. Some were actually **crying** they were so happy.

Finn suddenly remembered his mother's words, "Your life will change in many ways, and not all of them may be good." For the first time, he was beginning to understand that being a Maker would mean a lot more than getting to fly whenever you wanted. It would mean that from now on his life would never be the same.

But for that moment, with one hand holding his sister's and the other holding their trophy, surrounded by smiles and cheers, Finn did not care what the future held. When it came, he would be ready. For now, he was happy. That was enough.

## ABOUT THE AUTHOR

Sarah Aghajanian M.S.Ed., has been a classroom and reading teacher for over ten years. She attended Swarthmore College and received her master's degree from Bank Street in New York City. She is dedicated to creating a joyful classroom community where differences of all kinds are supported and celebrated. She lives in Philadelphia with her husband and new baby.

Manufactured by Amazon.com
Columbia, SC
31 March 2017